Rosie Raccoon's Rock and Roll Raft

by Barbara deRubertis • illustrated by R.W. Alley

THE KANE PRESS / NEW YORK

Alpha Betty's Class

Alexander Anteater

Bobby Baboon

Corky Cub

Dilly Dog

Eddie Elephant

Frances Frog

Gertie Gorilla

Hanna Hippo

Izzy Impala

Jeremy Jackrabbit

Kylie Kangaroo

Lana Llama

Maxwell Moose

Nina Nandu

Oliver Otter

Polly Porcupine

Quentin Quokka

STAR of the BOOK

Rosie Raccoon

Sammy Skunk

Tessa Tiger

Umma Ungka

Victor Vicuna

Walter Warthog

Xavier Ox

Yoko Yak

Zachary Zebra

Alpha Betty

Library of Congress Cataloging-in-Publication Data

deRubertis, Barbara.
Rosie Raccoon's rock and roll raft / by Barbara deRubertis ; illustrated by R.W. Alley.
p. cm. — (Animal antics A to Z)
Summary: Rosie Raccoon builds a raft for the Rocky River Raft Race, and remembers
her love of rock and roll to help her through the rapids.
ISBN 978-1-57565-339-6 (library binding : alk. paper) — ISBN 978-1-57565-330-3 (pbk. : alk. paper)
[1. Rafting (Sports)—Fiction. 2. Rafts—Fiction. 3. Racing—Fiction. 4. Raccoon—Fiction. 5. Alphabet.]
I. Alley, R. W. (Robert W.), ill. II. Title.
PZ7.D4475Ro 2011
[E]—dc22   2010025291

1 3 5 7 9 10 8 6 4 2

First published in the United States of America in 2011 by Kane Press, Inc.
Printed in the United States of America
WOZ0111

Series Editor: Juliana Hanford
Book Design: Edward Miller

Animal Antics A to Z is a registered trademark of Kane Press, Inc.

www.kanepress.com

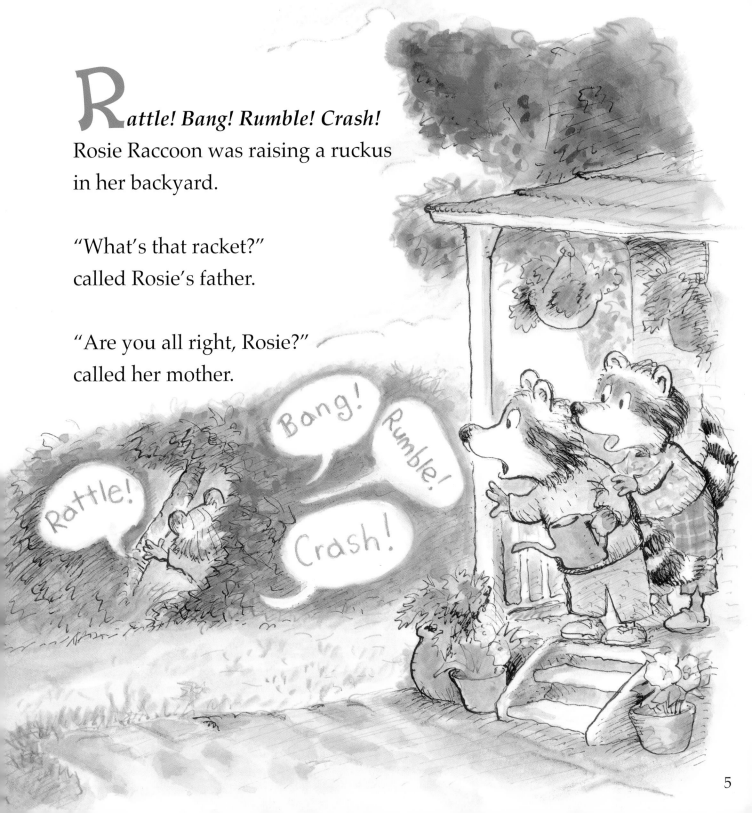

Rattle! Bang! Rumble! Crash!
Rosie Raccoon was raising a ruckus
in her backyard.

"What's that racket?"
called Rosie's father.

"Are you all right, Rosie?"
called her mother.

Rosie ran to her parents.
She was grubby. She was grimy.
Her shorts were ripped. Her shirt was torn.

But she was grinning from ear to ear.

"I'm building a RAFT," she reported.

"And I have to work FAST!
The Rocky River Raft Race is in four days!
Three of my friends are building rafts, too.
Everyone in Alpha Betty's class will be there!"

"No wonder you're in such a hurry,"
said Rosie's father.

"Is there any way we can help?"
asked Rosie's mother.

"Thanks for offering," said Rosie.
"But the rule is that kids must build
their OWN rafts.

Now I really need to get back to work!"
Rosie said, rushing away.

For the next three days, Rosie worked hard.
She tied logs together with rope.
She hammered boards across the logs.
And she made an oar.

All the while, she listened to her favorite
music—*rock and roll*!

The afternoon before the race, Rosie was
ready to give her raft a name.

"My raft will *rock* over the river rocks and
roll through the rapids!" she said proudly.

Grinning, Rosie painted a bright red sign:
Rosie's Rock and Roll Raft.

To celebrate, Rosie's parents surprised
her with her favorite supper:
roasted red peppers with rice
and carrot muffins with raisins.

They all sat on Rosie's raft while they ate.

And Rosie could not have been happier.

But when Rosie woke up the next morning,
she was terrified.

"What if I drop my oar?" she thought.
"What if I get stuck on the rocks?
What if I fall off my raft?"

"Don't worry," said Rosie's parents.
"You are READY for this race!
Just have fun—and remember to
rock and roll!"

Rosie and her parents drove to the river in her father's trusty old truck.

Rocky River Raft
Race Starts
HERE!

Alpha Betty, the rest of the class, and some parents were gathering on the shore.

The other rafters had already arrived.
They were pushing their rafts into the water.

Jeremy Jackrabbit had a NARROW raft.

Gertie Gorilla had a 𝔽𝔸ℕ𝒞𝒴 raft.

Oliver Otter had a **ROUND** raft.

Rosie looked at her raft. It was **STRONG**.

She smiled. Then she repeated to herself,
"Just have fun—and remember to
rock and roll!"

Rudy Rooster called the racers to the starting line. "Remember to watch out for Roller Coaster Rapids!" he warned.

"Now. . . . Ready! Set! Rock-a-doodle-DO!"

The race was on!

20

Everyone ran along the riverbank, cheering loudly.

Over and over, Alpha Betty called out, "Remember Roller Coaster Rapids! Be careful!"

Jeremy rowed so fast, his oar was a blur.
Gertie used her oar to push away from rocks.
Oliver tried to keep from spinning around.

Rosie was far behind them. She muttered,
"My raft is *strong*—but I need to go *faster*!"

Then they arrived at Roller Coaster Rapids.
The roaring, rushing water bounced the rafts
up and down. What a rough and rowdy ride!
It really WAS like a roller coaster!

Suddenly Jeremy dropped his oar.

Gertie got stuck in branches near the shore.

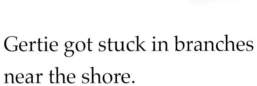

Oliver's raft was spinning around and around in a whirlpool. He got so dizzy, he fell OFF!

Everyone helped rescue the stranded rafters.
Then Alpha Betty called out, "Where's Rosie?"

Rosie's raft was stuck on a rock!
"Now what should I do?" she wondered.

Rosie thought quickly.
"I know! It's time to *rock and roll*!"

Carefully, Rosie began to rock and roll.
Back and forth. Back and forth.

CREEEEK! The raft lurched forward.

Rosie was in the race again!

Rosie rocked around the other rocks.
She rolled through the rest of the rapids.

And then she saw it—the red ribbon at the
finish line!

Rosie raised her oar above her head.
And she broke the red paper ribbon!

Everyone chanted, "Ro-sie! Ro-sie! Ro-sie!"

Her proud parents helped pull her raft to the side of the river. Rosie grinned at them.
"You were right," she said.
"All I had to do was *rock and roll*!"

Then Rosie Raccoon and her friends did a *ROCKIN'* victory dance on ***Rosie's Rock and Roll Raft***!

FUN FACTS

- Home: Raccoons are native to both North and South America. They live in wooded areas—and also in cities!
- Appearance: Raccoons are easily recognized by their black face masks and the black rings on their tails.
- Favorite foods: Raccoons like many different kinds of food, including nuts, fruits, insects, worms, fish . . . and garbage!
- **Did You Know?** Raccoons' front feet look a little like human hands. They can use them to open jars, trash cans, and even doors!

Reminder: Be sure not to approach or feed wild animals.

LOOK BACK

Learning to identify letter sounds (phonemes) at the beginning, middle, and end of words is called "phonemic awareness."

- The word *raft* <u>begins</u> with the *r* sound. Listen to the words on page 5 being read again. When you hear a word that <u>begins</u> with the *r* sound, rattle a shaker (made with rice or dry beans in a jar).
- The word *oar* <u>ends</u> with the *r* sound. Listen to the words on pages 8 being read again. When you hear a word that <u>ends</u> with the *r* sound, rattle your shaker!
- **Challenge**: Listen to the words on page 15 being read aloud. When a word has the *r* sound in the <u>middle</u>, rattle your shaker!

TRY THIS!

Build a RAFT of Words with Rosie Raccoon!

- Draw a raft with three side-by-side boards.*
- In the middle of the first board, write a green *r*. In the middle of the second board, write a red *a*. And in the middle of the third board, draw an **empty black circle**.
- On a piece of blank paper, draw 5 **black circles** (the same size as the one you drew on the raft). Cut out the circles and write one of these **black consonants** in each circle: *g, m, n, p, t.*
- Now you're ready to make words! Place a **black consonant** in the empty raft circle. Sound out the word. What does it mean? Continue making words using each of the **black consonants**!

*A printable, ready-to-use activity page with a raft picture is available at: www.kanepress.com/AnimalAntics/RosieRaccoon.html

FOR MORE ACTIVITIES, go to Rosie Raccoon's website: www.kanepress.com/AnimalAntics/RosieRaccoon.html
You'll also find a recipe for Rosie Raccoon's Rockin' Rigatoni!